Tomcat Takes a Walk

For all my cats and many thanks
to Alastair

Copyright © 1997 by Pippa Unwin
This special paperback edition first published in 2003 by Andersen Press Ltd.
The rights of Pippa Unwin to be identified as the author and illustrator of this work
have been asserted by her in accordance with the Copyright, Designs and Patents Act, 1988.
First published in Great Britain in 1997 by Andersen Press Ltd. 20 Vauxhall Bridge Road, London SW1V 2SA.
Published in Australia by Random House Australia Pty., 20 Alfred Street, Milsons Point, Sydney, NSW 2061.
All rights reserved. Colour separated in Italy by Fotoriproduzioni Grafiche, Verona.
Printed and bound in China.

10 9 8 7 6 5 4 3 2 1

British Library Cataloguing in Publication Data available.

ISBN 1 84270 195 9

This book has been printed on acid-free paper

Tomcat Takes a Walk

Story and pictures by Pippa Unwin

A

Andersen Press • London

Monday

Tomcat lives with Taffy in a cottage by the river.

But one day...

...Taffy packs her clothes into a big suitcase.

Where is she going?

Tomcat follows Taffy along the river path.

Then, Taffy is whisked away by a big, noisy, scary monster!

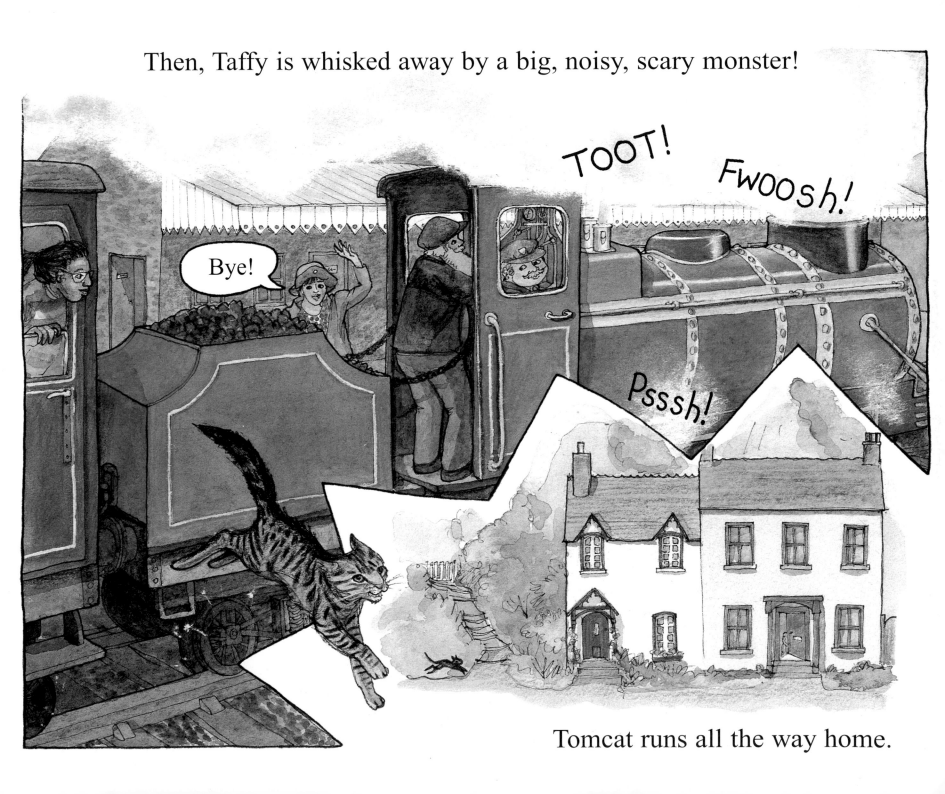

Tomcat runs all the way home.

Tuesday

Tomcat is lonely without Taffy.
Who's that walking past?

Nice pusscat.

Tomcat follows the walkers to the teashop.

…then he feels sleepy.

What a cosy bed!

It's time to go home…

This bag feels very heavy.

…along the river path.

As they pass Taffy's house, Tomcat wakes up…

Ooh!

wriggle jiggle

…and gives everyone a surprise!

Wednesday

The fishman comes today with food for Tomcat.

Tomcat goes with him on his rounds.

They visit the shop and Tomcat tries his first sugar mouse.

Outside, the door of the post van is open. Tomcat hops in.

There are letters to deliver.

Look who's in the bag!

TOMCAT
1 Riverside
Cottages

Tomcat is delivered home with the letters.

Thursday

This canoe looks perfect for a snooze. But now poor Tomcat's feeling a little seasic

As soon as he can, he leaps out...

Splash!

Silly Tomcat's dripping wet.

And he is on the wrong side of the river!

Miaow.

How can he get across? The train shows him the way.

It's that cat again.

Friday

After breakfast, Tomcat finds somewhere to sleep.

Let's go and fetch your sister from school.

Cat.

Are you a cat today, Billy?

Cat.

Tomcat wakes up in the playground. The children are very surprised to see him.

And Tomcat is very surprised to see them!

Tomcat tries to slip away, but he can't find anywhere to hide.

Tomcat goes home in Polly's bicycle basket.

Saturday

Tomcat can smell something fishy. All along the river people are fishing.

It is a competition to see who can catch the largest fish.

FISH SCALES

Mine's the heaviest!

Hey! Come back!

Tomcat has caught the biggest fish! Naughty Tomcat!

Cup of tea, dear?

MAGPIE

He jumps onto a boat to escape.

And he jumps off again when he reaches his house.

Sunday

Tomcat is asleep.
He's had a busy week. He wakes up to see a man walking past with a big dog.

The dog pulls free and chases Tomcat all the way to the railway station.

-SHOP-POST OFFICE-